Jonathan Liu.

STEP BY STEP

A linked series of Board Books, Concept Books and Story Books
for the pre-school child

Text copyright © 1988 by Diane Wilmer
Illustrations copyright © 1988 by Nicola Smee
First published 1988 by William Collins Sons & Company Ltd.
in association with The Albion Press Ltd.

Aladdin Books
Macmillan Publishing Company
866 Third Avenue, New York, NY 10022

First Aladdin Books edition 1988

Printed in Hong Kong

10   9   8   7   6   5   4   3   2   1

Library of Congress Cataloging-in-Publication Data

Wilmer, Diane.
  Over the wall.

  (Step by step)
  Summary: Nicky and Dan kick their ball across the
wall into Mrs. Wood's garden and worry how to get it
back.
  Reprint. Originally published: London: Collins, 1987.
  [1. Neighborliness—Fiction]   I. Smee, Nicola, ill.
II. Title.   III. Series: Step by step (New York, N.Y.)
PZ7.W6850   1988   [E]   88–16664
ISBN 0–689–71249–9

STEP BY STEP

Over the Wall

Diane Wilmer
illustrated by Nicola Smee

Aladdin Books
MACMILLAN PUBLISHING COMPANY
NEW YORK

It was Dan who kicked the ball
into Mrs. Wood's yard.
"Oh no!" he yelled. "*Now* what do we do?"
"We'll go over the wall," said Nicky.

It was a long way up, but Dan
climbed on Nicky's back.
Then Nicky scrambled up.

They sat on the wall and
looked for the ball.
They didn't see Mrs. Wood
weeding her garden, but
they did see the ball.
"Let's go!" shouted Nicky.

They landed SMACK! in the
middle of Mrs. Wood's flowers.

"Just what do you think you're doing?" she cried.
"Sorry, Mrs. Wood," said Nicky.
"Our ball's in your yard."

"Never mind your ball.
Look what you've done to
my flowers!" snapped Mrs. Wood.
"Get out of my garden this minute.
Go on — now!"

The boys hurried home.
"Now what?" moaned Dan.
"We'll have to go back,"
said Nicky.
"Go back over the wall?"
asked Dan. "What about
Mrs. Wood?"

"We'll wait for her to go
out," whispered Nicky.
"Then we'll sneak over there."

They hid in the bushes and
waited and waited.
Dan yawned.
"This is boring."
"Ssshhh!" hissed Nicky.

When Mrs. Wood went out,
they went in.

But the ball was gone.

Dan looked under the bushes,
it was dark and damp down there.
Spiders crept around his face,
and branches tickled his hair.
"OH! I don't like this."
And he shivered.

Nicky tiptoed down the path and
peeked in the shed.
A blackbird flew out, squawking
at him.
"Help!" yelled Nicky, and ran back
up the path. . .

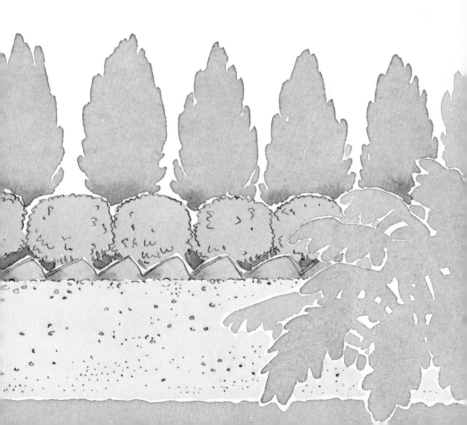

Right into Dan!

"Let's get out of here!"
cried Dan.

And they ran through the
gate as fast as their legs
could take them.

"Whew! I'm glad
we're home."

Then Nicky saw *h*
Mrs. Wood, talking
to his mom in the kitchen
They tried to sneak upstairs
but Mom spotted them.
"Come here," she called.
"Mrs. Wood wants to talk to you."

"We're very, very sorry," said the boys.

Mrs. Wood stopped them.

"So am I," she said. "I was rude to both of you.
Here, I've brought back your ball."

"Oh, thank you!" said Nicky and Dan.

"Thank you very much."

"That's all right," said Mrs. Wood.

"Come over later and have some ice cream."

It was nice in Mrs. Wood's garden,
all quiet and peaceful.
"I like it here," said Nicky.

"I'm glad," said Mrs. Wood.
"Come over again soon – both of you."